THE BLACK CAULDRON STORY BOOK

Taran longed to be a hero, and not a pig-keeper, but he
quickly found that adventures weren't what he had imagined.
His pig, Hen Wen, could show the dreadful Horned King where
the Black Cauldron was – and the King must never find it,
for if he did, he could raise an army of the dead and with
it rule the world.

Trying to save Hen Wen from the Horned King, Taran tries to
find the Black Cauldron himself, in order to destroy it.
He's helped by Princess Eilonwy, Flewddur the old minstrel,
and the little wood creature Gurgi. But in the
desolate Marshes of Morva, Taran finds that the Cauldron's
powers can only be stopped by someone climbing into
the Cauldron. And whoever does so will never come out alive …
Taran and his friends must be brave and determined as
they try to fulfil their task, for the Horned King will
stop at nothing to achieve his ends.

The Black Cauldron

Storybook written by Alison Sage

Hippo Books
Scholastic Publications Limited
London

Scholastic Publications Ltd.,
10 Earlham Street, London WC2H 9LN, UK

Scholastic Inc.,
730 Broadway, New York, NY 10003, USA

Scholastic Tab Publications Ltd.,
123 Newkirk Road, Richmond Hill,
Ontario L4C 3G5, Canada

Ashton Scholastic Pty. Ltd.,
PO Box 579, Gosford, New South Wales,
Australia

Ashton Scholastic Ltd.,
165 Marua Road, Panmure, Auckland 6,
New Zealand

First published in the United Kingdom
by Scholastic Publications Ltd., 1985
Walt Disney Pictures presents THE BLACK CAULDRON
Produced in association with Silver Screen Partners II
Based on *The Chronicles of Prydain* series by Lloyd Alexander
Music by Elmer Bernstein
Distributed by Buena Vista Distribution Co. Inc.
Copyright 1985 © Walt Disney Productions,
ISBN 0 590 70419 2

Legend has it that there was once a king so cruel and evil that even the gods feared him. Since no prison could hold him, he was thrown alive into a crucible of molten iron. There his demonic spirit was imprisoned forever in the form of a great, Black Cauldron. In revenge, he cursed, "My power will not die: whosoever uses the Black Cauldron for evil will be all-powerful, for my blood will flow with his and together we will either rule the world or destroy it!"

This, however, was a long, long time ago. Many now doubted that it had ever happened. Did the Cauldron still exist? Or had it been lost in the mists of time – hidden, perhaps by the Fairfolk, those small, friendly spirits who loved peace and hated evil? Or had it been destroyed by its own black powers?

It was then, at this time, that fear again came to the green fields and hills of the country of Prydain. The Horned King, one of the Old Ones of Cryador, had set up his court in the ancient Castle of Cares. Its iron gates were now closed and the land around was bare and deserted. Terrible stories were told of travellers in that region who had vanished without trace and now no one willingly went near.

These stories had even reached the ears of Dallben, an old hero who had fought in the wars with Cryador. He now lived peacefully in a little cottage at Caer Dallben. He was one of the few humans to have friends amongst the Fairfolk. He had knowledge, too, of the inheritance of Prydain and the Dark Past of Cryador. To Taran, who lived with him, he was a kindly but strict old man who had been like a father to him. Taran could not imagine him in anything but his old brown slippers and jerkin. Had he really once worn the armour of Prydain and ridden the horse Cloud Spirit? All he seemed to wield nowadays was a bread knife, and his chief interest, after Taran, was stroking the cat and looking after Hen Wen the pig.

One sunny morning, however, all this began to change. Dallben was getting breakfast, but something was bothering him. He sensed that somewhere, somehow, forces of evil were stirring.

"I haven't seen the Fairfolk for months," he muttered, "and these stories of the Horned King. . . If it is true about Castle Cares. . ." He put the bread on the table. Griff, the cat, rubbed against his knees. "Hmm, yes, I know. You want your breakfast, don't you? But just let me think a little. This is important."

The pot on the fire hissed and spluttered as Hen Wen's porridge boiled over. "Taran!" shouted Dallben. "The porridge! TARAN!" Taran stood by the window, looking out, a faraway expression on his face.

"Sorry Dallben," he said, suddenly waking up. "Only, I was wondering if there was really going to be war, will it be over before I get a chance to fight?"

Dallben looked serious. "Best thing if it is," he said. "The only good war is one that's over. Now, you listen to me. . . The Horned King..."

"I'm not afraid of him," interrupted Taran, scooping porridge into Hen Wen's dish.

"Well, then you're a fool," said Dallben. "And mind that porridge – Look!" Taran, careless in his anger, slopped some on his hand. "You'll have more to worry about than burned fingers, I can promise you, if the Horned King is really preparing for war."

"Ouch! But why do I have to spend my time looking after a stupid pig? I should be learning to fight," said Taran, his eyes flashing rebelliously.

"Taran!" said Dallben. "There's plenty of work to do, so get on with it!" Taran left, his shoulders squared in defiance, his chin held high and angry.

It was so hard. He wasn't a child anymore. Could Dallben not see that? It was time for him to be a hero, not a pig keeper. Crossly he kicked Hen Wen's breakfast into her little house. It shot out again, followed by Hen Wen's pretty little pink nose and a pair of reproachful blue eyes. Taran felt a bit mean, but he was still angry. He picked up a stick and waved it like a sword. Hen Wen scurried behind a barrel. She looked so bewildered that Taran had to laugh. Waving his stick, he charged a flock of geese, which scattered in a confusion of feathers and angry squawks.

"Look, Hen Wen!" he shouted, "The hero Taran fights all the enemies of Prydain. Even the Horned King." This last was addressed to Dallben's goat, which peered out, curious at the commotion. "Run, you coward," shouted Taran joyfully. The goat promptly slipped round behind Taran and charged.

"I'm the – ooof," said Taran. His victory shout was suddenly cut short as the goat sent him straight over Hen Wen and into a muddy puddle. "Ooh," moaned Taran, play-acting. "So young to die." Poor Hen Wen, puzzled and upset, nuzzled his cheek. Taran giggled.

"Taran!" said Dallben sternly. "Is this how a hero behaves?"

"It was a joke," said Taran uncomfortably, "and anyway, why should I have to spend my life as an assistant pig-keeper?"

"Listen, Taran, be patient. Your time will come. Now wash Hen Wen, because she's covered in mud."

Taran sighed and did as he was told. He was very fond of the pretty little pig and normally they were the best of friends. "Now for your bath, Hen," he said. "I just wish Dallben could understand. I am old enough now to – hey! What's the matter?" Suddenly Hen Wen stiffened in terror and tried to leap out of her bath. "Whoa! Hen, whoa!" shouted Taran, as the little pig jumped into his arms, shaking with fright.

Dallben took one look at Hen Wen and his manner changed completely. "Quickly, bring her inside, Taran. Evil times have come quicker than I imagined."

He filled a pail of water and carefully lit several candles around it. He smiled rather sadly. "What you are about to see belongs to the ancient past of Prydain and also to her future. You must never reveal the secret of Hen Wen's powers to anyone. There is always someone ready to seize the Old Magic and use it for evil."

"Evil? Powers? Hen Wen is only a pig. . .I don't understand," said Taran, bewildered.

But Dallben had already begun the Magic. He swirled the water in the pail with his staff and in a sing song voice began chanting.

"Hen Wen from you I do beseech
The knowledge that lies
   beyond my reach.
Troubled thoughts weigh on your heart.
Pray now these thoughts impart."

The candles flickered, and quietly Hen Wen dipped her nose into the spinning water, which began to glow softly. Suddenly the water became troubled and a figure could be seen. It became sharp and clear.

"The Horned King!" said Dallben. "I thought as much."

The picture changed. Creatures like giant pterodactyls stood out blackly against a pale sky. "What are *those?*" cried Taran.

"Gwythaints. . .now shh," warned Dallben.

The picture changed once more to reveal the Black Cauldron. Dallben grimaced. "Now I understand," he said slowly. "The Horned King is looking for the Black Cauldron and he has sent out the Gwythaints. In his hands, the Black Cauldron will become a terrible weapon. Nothing could stand against its power."

"Look!" said Taran, "there's Hen Wen," as the pig's own reflection appeared in the water.

"Things are worse than I thought," muttered Dallben. "We have not much time left."

The vision stopped as suddenly as it began. Dallben started packing food into a bag. "You must leave *at once*. Take Hen Wen to the hidden cottage at the edge of the forest where we stayed last summer and remain there until I come for you."

"But why must I hide?" asked Taran.

"The Horned King has discovered Hen Wen's powers," said Dallben, gravely. "We must make sure he never uses them to find the Black Cauldron. Now hurry, and remember, untried courage alone is no match for the Horned King. You must take care." He hugged Taran fiercely.

"I won't fail you," said Taran bravely, patting Hen Wen.

He smiled as he went out of the farmyard, in spite of the seriousness of the situation. It was his first real adventure, his first trip alone outside Caer Dallben, and he was excited. "We'll show Dallben, won't we Hen Wen?" he whispered to the little pig.

It was a bright, clear morning as Taran and Hen Wen set off for the forest. Taran was happy. It was good to be out on the road, with the sun in his face and the nice, friendly little pig as his companion. How could there be any danger in these peaceful green fields?

Soon the pair reached the forest and Taran found a stream. Greedily, Hen Wen dipped in her little pink snout to drink and suddenly a vision appeared on the water – a vision of Taran as a warrior! A voice called softly, "Taran! Taran, hero; the greatest warrior in all Prydain. . ."

"Hen, look!" said Taran, and turned to Hen Wen. But the pig had disappeared. "Hen!" shouted Taran, suddenly scared, "Where are you? Don't tease me."

There was no trace of the little pig. His heart thumping fiercely, Taran ran amongst the trees, searching for his friend. Suddenly, the friendly green depths seemed threatening. Leaves rustled behind a bush. "Hen?" called Taran, a slight trembling in his voice. There was no answer. Taran took out an apple and walked towards the bush.

Crash! Something heavy landed on Taran's shoulders. Startled, he overbalanced and fell, dropping the apple. Chuckling with glee, the creature which had attacked him leapt after it. "Yaaa," gurgled the creature. "Give poor starving Gurgi munchings and crunchings . . . nice apple. . ."

Taran lay on the ground, bewildered. Gurgi polished the apple on his fur, humming happily and opened his mouth to take a bite.

Taran was now more angry than afraid and he made a grab for the apple. "Hey, you little hairy thief! That's my apple – Yow!" Gurgi bit Taran smartly on the finger and scampered off into the bushes. "Give it back!" shouted Taran. "Now!" Gurgi crept out, sniffed the red, juicy fruit longingly, and gave Taran a sad, beseeching look like a puppy who wants a chocolate drop. But Taran was too angry to relent. "Come on. . ." he said warningly. Gurgi took a quick look at Taran, then at the apple, took a huge bite out of it and thrust it all wet and dribbly into Taran's outstretched hand.

"Ugh! you horrible, greedy little thing," cried Taran, and shook his fist at Gurgi, now cowering out of reach. Gurgi's big, blue eyes filled with tears.

"Oh! Oh!" he whimpered, "Gurgi always in trouble. No one love Gurgi. Never have any nice munchings and crunchings. Oh. . .*sniff*. . .don't be cross with Gurgi."

"Stop snivelling," said Taran crossly. "I'm not going to smack you. Now, listen. Have you seen a little pig?"

Gurgi looked up eagerly. "Pink, pretty pig?" he said, still keeping out of Taran's reach. "Curly tail?"

"Yes, yes!" said Taran excitedly. Gurgi suddenly looked dejected.

"No - no - no. Gurgi not see piggy."

Taran's face fell and he pushed Gurgi away.

"What's the use of asking a creature like you?" he said. Gurgi trotted after him.

"Please, please, yes, Gurgi remembers! Gurgi sees piggy run through forest. Clever Gurgi. Mmm, yes, Gurgi did see, he really did. . ." He grabbed Taran's hand. "Follow Gurgi; we will find the lost piggy." He discovered a lump in Taran's pocket which was the apple. "Gurgi find munchings and crunchings here somewhere. . ."

Suddenly a dreadful squealing came from the nearby clearing. "Hen Wen!" shouted Taran, racing towards the cries. There in front of him was poor Hen Wen, running for her life, while the Gwythaints in the sky circled waiting to pounce, their cruel talons outstretched. Taran felt a rushing of air, heard the rustling of wind through a million scales as a Gwythaint swooped. Hen Wen wheeled and dodged, kicking the earth in the face of her pursuer. Blinded, the Gwythaint had to fly upwards or risk crashing to the ground. A second Gwythaint swooped to attack. Taran leapt forward, but the creature was swifter. Like a giant bird of prey, it scooped up the shrieking Hen Wen in its talons, knocking Taran to the ground with a leathery wing. Taran clutched at its tail, but the first creature joined the attack and he was beaten off, half stunned.

Victorious, the Gwythaints soared into the sky, with Hen Wen. Taran ran after them screaming desperately, "Come back! Come back!"

His face and arms were scratched with

brambles, his legs like jelly, but still he ran through the trees towards a high cliff. Sobbing with effort he struggled upwards, stones tumbling around him, until he reached the top. At last he could see the Gwythaints, tiny silhouettes against the sky, heading towards the dark shape of the Castle

of the Horned King. "I'll get you back, Hen Wen, I swear it," he said determinedly.

Just then a timid paw brushed his hand.

"No. . . not go in there. Gurgi says forget the piggy. . ."

Taran jumped. "What are you doing here?" he said angrily as he saw Gurgi.

"Gurgi wants to be your friend."

"Friend! You must be joking. All you did back there was run away. I don't have cowards for friends." Taran turned away contemptuously. "I'm going to rescue Hen Wen from the Castle of the Horned King. I don't suppose you're coming?"

Gurgi shrank back. In the distance lightning flashed over the dark outline of the castle and they could faintly hear the rumble of thunder. "Well?" demanded Taran, his voice trembling slightly in spite of himself.

"No - no - no," whispered Gurgi. "Terrible place for Gurgi."

"Just as I thought," said Taran. "You're a coward. Here–" and he handed Gurgi the apple, "you can have this if it's what you want." He turned determinedly towards the castle, and set off without a backwards glance. Gurgi sniffled miserably.

"Alone. Gurgi alone. If Taran go into the evil castle, will he ever return?"

Although he had sounded so brave to Gurgi, Taran could not help shivering as he approached the dark fortress. It was silent, as if waiting for something. For him? Taran shook himself sharply. "Stop thinking like that!" he muttered.

He scrambled as quietly as he could over the rocks at the foot of the castle. It was eerie. Not a single living thing had he seen since he left Gurgi. All around him, thunder rumbled ominously. He took a deep breath and started to climb the castle wall. It was easier than he had expected, for there were little cracks between the blocks and he inched his way up patiently. He was tired, however, and at a particularly sharp crack of thunder, he missed his footing and slipped. Desperately he clawed at the stones, but they fell away from him. He struggled to keep his balance and suddenly he realized that he was looking at a small opening in the castle wall. His tiredness forgotten, he tore at the leaves and creepers. He could see a faint light coming from the inside.

He scrambled through the hole and edged cautiously along a dim corridor. From the direction of the light came an intermittent rumbling sound, like a distant drill. Taran froze. He crept forward to the lighted doorway and peered round. A huge guard sat slumped over a table, snoring. "One of the Horned King's henchmen," thought Taran, his heart thumping. As quietly as a cat, he slipped past the sleeper, terrified that at any minute he would stir and sound the alarm. A chain rattled and, snarling viciously, a dog hurled himself at Taran, who shrank back into the shadows. The henchman half woke and angrily shouted at the dog. "What's the matter? Get back before I give you something to make a noise about, you stupid brute." Then he stretched, yawning. "Time to make our rounds, I suppose," he said, and dragged the dog, still whining, off down the corridor.

Taran's legs could hardly move with fright, but he forced himself to slip through the door in front of him. He blinked at the sudden brightness. He was standing between two overhead beams in the roof of the main dining room. Below him, the Horned King's henchmen were eating and relaxing in drunken good humour.

A tankard clashed with another in a toast and an out-of-tune fiddle played for a plump, red-faced girl dancing on the table.

The captain grinned and blew a noisy kiss at the girl. A couple of Gwythaints snarled and snapped at each other at the far end of the hall, quarrelling over huge lumps of meat. Taran could hear a splintering sound as their teeth crunched through bone.

Directly below him, a small, evil-looking dwarf hopped onto a barrel and tried to snatch a piece of meat that the captain had been saving for himself. "Hands off, Creeper!" said the captain, unpleasantly, and he speared the meat with his own knife. Creeper slid off the barrel with an empty plate and the guards laughed coarsely as he scurried away like a frightened snake.

A cold wind blew through the hanging curtains and Taran shuddered. The guards' drunken laughter died away. Stupidly, they stared at one another as the candles flickered. A dog howled, dismally afraid, and even the Gwythaints cowered on the floor, their half-chewed bones forgotten. Taran strained his eyes in the darkness. What was this approaching evil? CRACK! He leapt back as a ball of fire exploded beneath him. Flames licked the rafters and

20

white smoke curled through the hall. The guards huddled together like chickens as through the smoke, a pair of horns could be seen. Slowly, the smoke cleared, and outlined against the archway stood the towering figure of the Horned King. Horned King.

A gasp of horror passed round the room, like a rustle of dead leaves, and the Horned King's eyes flashed brilliant green. Creeper, the dwarf, wormed his way to his master's feet. "Welcome, welcome, Your Majesty," he murmured. "We were just celebrating our successful mission – uh – I mean, we were drinking to *your* success, my lord." He giggled evilly. "Bring in the prisoner."

A door opened at the end of the hall and a guard came in dragging poor Hen Wen, terrified and whimpering. "A bowl of water. Quickly!" ordered Creeper. "This, my lord, is the pig that can create visions."

The Horned King's face was white and cold. "Show His Majesty where the Black Cauldron can be found," purred Creeper confidently.

Hen Wen blinked her blue eyes and turned her little pink snout away. "Go on!" urged Creeper harshly, a note of anxiety creeping into his voice. "Show it!"

The Horned King leaned forward and grabbed him, talon-like fingers tightening around the dwarf's neck. "*Aaagh!*" screamed Creeper. The Horned King pushed him away. The dwarf turned to Hen Wen and his voice took on a new edge. "Listen, piggy, His Majesty wants that Cauldron. He wants it *now;* and his patience is very short."

Deliberately he sidled over to a burning brazier where a pair of iron tongs were glowing white hot. Taran, who had seen all this from the rafters, gasped in horror. Surely, they weren't going to torture poor Hen Wen? "No!" he cried. "Leave her alone!" and before he had quite worked out what he was going to do, he found himself tumbling through the air. He seized a hanging tapestry to break his fall – and then he was lying bruised, but unhurt in the middle of the floor. He leapt to his feet and grabbed a stick as the guards ran forward to seize him.

"Don't you dare touch Hen Wen or I'll – Oh!" Taran lashed out at the first guard with his stick, only to see it slashed in two as easily as a poppy stalk. The guards pinned his arms behind his back and he had given himself up for dead when he heard the Horned King's voice, "Release him!" He fell next to Hen Wen, who greeted him with a joyful squeal.

The Horned King stared at them both coldly. "Boy, I imagine that you are the keeper of this pig?" Taran nodded, fearfully.

"Answer the King when he talks to you," said Creeper malevolently, giving him a poke.

"Then you will tell her to show me where to find the Black Cauldron," continued the Horned King, ignoring the dwarf.

"Oh, but I can't," cried Taran miserably. "I promised."

"In which case," said the Horned King in his hollow voice, "the pig is of no further use."

Creeper ran forward eagerly and dragged Hen Wen to a chopping block. A hooded guard stepped forward with a raised axe. Hen Wen gave one last sad squeal and covered her eyes.

"Stop! Stop!" cried Taran, sobbing. "I'll make her tell you what you want."

Almost crying with helplessness, Taran knelt over the pan of water and began to recite the words of the ancient spell:

"Hen Wen from you I do beseech
Knowledge that lies beyond my reach."

The water glowed and then slowly the picture cleared and the image of a huge, black cauldron appeared on the water.

"So," said the Horned King, rising from his throne, his eyes glowing. "It does still exist. . ." He trembled as if burning with a terrible passion. "Show me where it is!"

Taran looked up to see the Horned King towering over him. He lost his head completely and shrieked in pure terror. Leaping wildly to his feet, he tripped over the pan of water. It splashed into the face of the Horned King, who recoiled with a ghastly scream, clutching desperately at his eyes.

Taran grabbed Hen Wen and ran through the archway behind the throne as pandemonium broke out. "After them, you clods!" screamed Creeper. "Catch them, or you'll suffer."

The Gwythaints beat their wings against their perch, uttering furious cries. Suddenly, the perch snapped and they joined the chase, dragging broken chains which tangled in the burning brazier, cascading white-hot coals in the path of the guards. The Gwythaints swooped to pounce; but their broken perch caught in the archway and they crashed to the ground. Taran fled, pulling Hen Wen after him.

Down the corridors they ran and through another doorway. Taran heaved the door shut and bolted it. The cool night air hit his face with reassuring freshness. He was on the castle walls. Gasping with effort, he picked up Hen Wen and ran to the parapet. Far below him, the moat sparkled peacefully in the moonlight.

"Be brave, Hen," whispered Taran, as he struggled to lift her over the wall. "It's our only chance."

Behind him, he could hear the sound of splintering wood, as the door quivered under the axes of the guards. "Swim, Hen! Swim!" he begged as with one last heave the little pig tumbled over the parapet towards the moat. He swung himself onto the wall.

"I'm coming – aah!" Creeper seized Taran's leg and he was dragged backwards into the arms of the guards.

"I caught him, Your Majesty," laughed Creeper, flushed with success.

"But you let the pig go!" hissed the Horned King. His claw-like hand grasped the dwarf by the throat.

"It wasn't my fault," Creeper gurgled, choking, as the Horned King sent him spinning to the floor.

"Throw the boy into the dungeon," commanded the King, and guards ran to do his bidding.

When he awoke the next morning, for a moment Taran thought he was still dreaming. Then, with dreadful clarity, he remembered the previous day. He was a prisoner, perhaps for ever, in the castle of the Horned King. A couple of fat tears slid down his cheek as he remembered his last, confident words to Dallben. "I will succeed. I *will!*" he muttered bitterly.

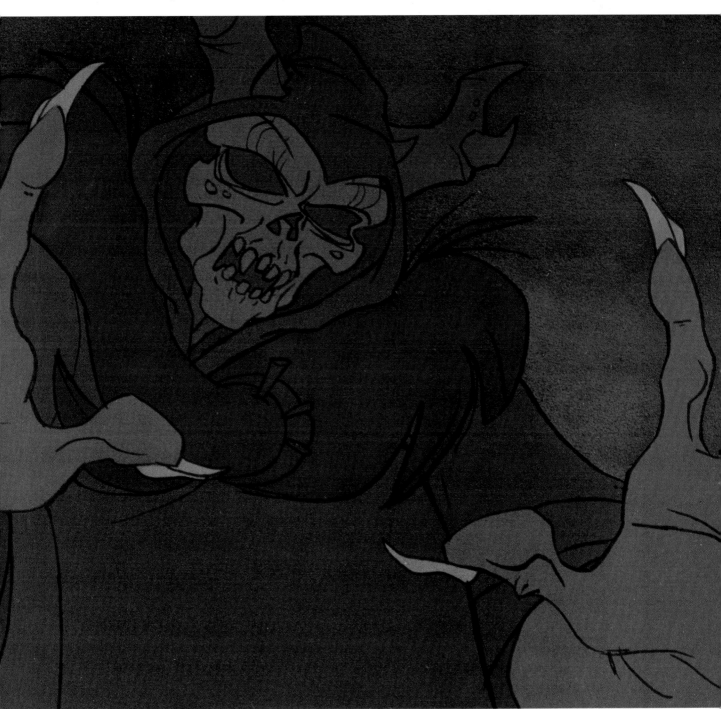

Suddenly, one of the stone flagstones in the floor began to move. Slowly it rose in the air and a faint glow appeared in the dark, square hole. Before Taran's astonished eyes a ball of light, irridescent like a soap bubble, rolled into his cell, followed by a girl of about his own age. "Oh, so there is someone in here," she said, smiling at him. "I'm Princess Eilonwy."

The bubble rolled over to him and cautiously, he touched it. It gleamed brilliant white and swished up into his face, as if to look at him more closely. "Oh," said Taran, "What is it?"

"It's magic," said Eilonwy, coolly. "You're a prisoner like I am, aren't you? The Horned King kidnapped me because he wanted my bubble. He wanted it to tell him about the Black Cauldron."

"That's why I'm here too," said Taran excitedly. "He wanted my pig, Hen Wen – she has visions – to show him where it was hidden." The bubble whirled past the two and down the hole in the floor.

"Come on," said Eilonwy. "We'd better go."

Down through the floor they went, and along a narrow, damp passage, lit only by the

26

light of the bubble. Rats scuffled noisily in the darkness as the bubble swooped on them, seemingly for the pleasure of seeing them run. Suddenly, chasing a particularly fat rat, the bubble squeezed through a hole in the side of the passage. "Come back here!" said Eilonwy, crossly. "It's always chasing – ugh!"

They peered through the hole, and in the dim light they could see that the bubble had entered a burial chamber. In the middle was a huge tomb, carved out of glassy black obsidian. Taran leaned against the wall, staring into the darkened chamber. "This

magnificently-wrought sword. Reverently, Taran lifted it down from its centuries-old resting place. "A great sword for a great hero," he said softly to himself as he stood admiring the workmanship of the handle

must be the tomb of the Old King, the lord of the castle before the Horned King," whispered Eilonwy. Taran felt the stones around him move as the wall crumbled and collapsed and he was thrown violently into the burial chamber. "Taran! Taran!" called Eilonwy, "Are you all right?"

Taran nodded and sneezed, his nose full of dust. He was at the foot of the tomb. Quietly, he scrambled to his feet and stared at the great, stone monument. Gold letters glittered all round the base, and something flashed brilliant red from the top of the tomb. It was a red stone in the handle of a

and the runic writing on the blade.

A rattle of wheels from the passage disturbed his thoughts. Someone was coming. Eilonwy and the bubble ducked into the safety of the chamber. Creeper was urging on several guards, who were dragging a heavily loaded cart. They paused, out of breath, while the dwarf unlocked the doors to a secret chamber. "A good lot this time," he crooned. "His Majesty will be pleased." The cartwheels slipped as they went into the chamber and a human hand fell out from under the heavy covers and trailed in the dust.

At that moment, the bubble began to get agitated. It swept up some stairs to another small doorway. Taran and Eilonwy could hear voices on the other side of the door.

"You're making a dreadful mistake," said someone with a strong accent. "I'm not a spy, I'm a bard."

Silence, except for the barking of a dog. "But I *am*. . ." went on the voice anxiously. "I sing songs about. . .men of action – like you, sir."

Taran and Eilonwy peered into the cell. One of the guards was tying up a new prisoner, an old poet, by the look of him. He looked scared.

"Oh dear," he said. "Oh, do be careful – these are the hands of an artist." The guard ignored him. "It may seem funny to you," and the poet let out a nervous giggle, "but I really didn't know who lived here. I promise you." The dog growled menacingly as the guard yanked him towards the door. "Don't you know who I am?" said the poet raising his voice slightly as the guard appeared about to leave. "I'm the great Flewddur Fflam, minstrel of minstrels –" The door slammed shut. "Balladeer to the grandest courts!" shouted Flewddur at the top of his voice. Then he looked down to the harp at his feet. "Well, I *am*," he said defensively. A string from the harp twanged and broke. "Uh, well, I'm sure to be invited soon. . ."

Taran and Eilonwy shivered with disgust and loathing, as they slipped past the chamber. Taran's sword rattled and Eilonwy raised a questioning eyebrow. Taran pointed to the burial chamber of the Warrior King and Eilonwy looked horrified. "We're going to need it," whispered Taran, little knowing how true these words were going to be.

His eye passed round the gloomy cell and suddenly he realized that he was not alone. He already shared the dungeon with a skeleton. "Oh help!! Great Beelin!" he yelled.

"Can we help?" interrupted Eilonwy politely. For once, Flewddur was too astonished to speak. Taran began to untie him while Eilonwy explained who they were. Just then, heavy footsteps could be heard running down the passageway. ". . .and now they know we've escaped, so hurry!" she finished.

They fled through the door and over a footbridge. Taran caught his foot on a nail and stumbled. The sword flew out of his hand and clattered noisily on the stones. He slipped under the bridge not a moment too soon as the guards pounded over the planks.

When the coast seemed clear, he cautiously climbed out. "Eilonwy," he whispered urgently.

"Pig boy!" came a coarse voice from behind, as a guard struck him on the shoulder, knocking him to the ground.

Taran looked up in time to see the guard raise his axe. Swiftly he rolled to one side. There was his sword! He snatched it up to parry the blow. He flinched, waiting for the guard to strike him, but *nothing happened!* The guard's axe had turned in his hand, and the man cowered, helpless. As Taran realized that it was the power of the sword in his hand, a broad smile spread across his face. "A warrior's sword! A warrior's sword!" he chanted, waving it proudly in the air.

"Taran!" whispered Eilonwy, "are you all right? Let's get out of here."

A voice yelled, "There they are!" and two guards leapt in pursuit, but one wave of Taran's sword sent them rolling in confusion. Eilonwy looked in awed astonishment at Taran, but he took her arm and they ran panting into the wine cellar.

"You go on, princess," he urged, "I've got an idea." Guards were pounding into the cellar as he split the casks. Soon men were slipping and sliding in all directions and crashing into each other in a flood of wine. "Don't drink too much," called Taran, as he ran laughing to join Eilonwy. But his smiles soon disappeared as they almost collided with a band of guards led by Creeper. Desperately, they doubled back and made for the drawbridge, only to see guards running towards them from all sides.

"Taran!" screamed Eilonwy, agonized.

The bridge was up. They were trapped. "Get them alive!" barked Creeper.

Taran raised his sword as Eilonwy flattened herself against the raised bridge. "We've got you now, pig boy," sneered Creeper. A spear flew through the air and bit into the bridge behind Eilonwy's head.

"Do something, Taran," she screamed. "Use the sword."

Taran looked at the steel links of the drawbridge chain. They were as thick as a man's thigh. Taking a deep breath he swung the sword at them. Electric sparks flew – and the chain severed like butter. It snaked up the wall, clanking furiously, and the huge bridge slowly began sliding towards the ground, leading the way to freedom.

The guards drew back in fear at the power of the sword. At this moment, Flewddur, with a dog snapping viciously at his heels, came running towards them. ′

"Make way for a mad dog, stand aside there!" he bawled and the bewildered guards obeyed blindly. The bridge hit the ground with a terrific crash.

"Run, princess, run!" shouted Taran. The portcullis, which would cut off the runaways from their pursuers, began sliding towards the ground, its spikes gleaming.

"Run Flewddur!" shouted Eilonwy. With its last effort the dog fixed its teeth in the seat of Flewddur's baggy trousers.

"Help!" yelled Flewddur, now having to do the running for two. Suddenly the dog looked up and saw the falling portcullis. It lost its nerve. Crash! The gate fell, ripping Flewddur's trousers and separating him from his four-legged pursuer. Quite confused, the dog growled, guarding his piece of Flewddur's trousers as if it was the Black Cauldron itself.

"Why didn't you – *puff* – tell us," said Flewddur, desperately trying to run holding up his trousers at the same time, "that – *pant* – you had a magic sword? It would have saved a lot of trouble. . ."

Creeper was terrified. He wriggled and cringed in a way that was unpleasant to watch. He knew that he had to tell the Horned King the news of Taran's escape, but as it happened, things did not turn out as he expected.

He crept up to the Horned King's private chamber.

"Sire," he mumbled. The Horned King spoke from the shadows.

"You have found the pig?"

Creeper gulped, "The pig-boy has escaped – but I'll strangle myself, I'll. . ."

The Horned King took no notice. He seemed to smile faintly.

"Good. He'll find the pig for us. Send the Gwythaints after the boy!"

Creeper stopped choking in amazement. Hardly able to believe his ears, he crawled out of his master's presence, mumbling apologies.

Unaware of the evil plans of the Horned King, Taran, Eilonwy and Flewddur were happily resting in a clearing in the forest. It seemed impossible that anything could hurt them in the sunny friendliness of the sheltering trees.

Taran was lovingly polishing his new sword, "I earned you," he whispered softly, "I earned a warrior's sword." Eilonwy offered to sew up Flewddur's trousers and Flewddur immediately began singing a heroic song about their exploits.

Would they flinch?
Would they falter?
No one step their course they alter," he sang.

Eilonwy giggled, impressed with his flow of words if not with his poetry.

"I hate sewing, really, Flewddur; but I hope this will hold until you get some more trousers." She handed them to him, suddenly serious.

"But Flewddur, weren't you a little scared back there?"

Flewddur threw out his chest proudly. "What me? A Fflam, frightened? I don't know the meaning of the word. I–" His harp twanged warningly and he laughed. "Well, er, yes, of course I was afraid."

Taran looked up. "I wasn't," he said coolly. Eilonwy was irritated at this.

"Don't be silly, of course you were."

"No I wasn't," retorted Taran. "No one could stand against me, could they, Flewddur? And, when I've found Hen Wen,

I'm going back to the castle to teach the Horned King a lesson."

"Indeed, you have a Sword of Power, and you are a mighty–"

"I think you are both powerfully stupid," said Eilonwy angrily.

Taran was furious that she wouldn't take him seriously. "I got us out of the castle."

"Your *sword* got us out of the castle," corrected Eilonwy, coldly.

"Only a great warrior could handle a sword of power, like this. And," he continued crushingly, "what does a girl know about swords?"

Eilonwy went pale. "If it wasn't for me, you'd still be in the Horned King's dungeon."

Flewddur had been watching them

argue with a troubled expression on his face. Vainly he tried to keep the peace. "Princess, please don't – Taran, you–"

But the princess was far too angry to listen and she brushed him aside.

"Yes, I am a princess, and that means I don't go around boasting all the time. You – you're just so *boring*."

Taran opened his mouth to reply and Flewddur said hastily, "Princess, listen. We must work together–"

"How dare you argue with me?" said Eilonwy. "Take your wretched trousers!" And she threw them at him and stormed off between the trees. Taran walked off in the opposite direction.

Flewddur sank down dejected. A few minutes passed. No one spoke. Taran walked back through the trees and there in front of him was Eilonwy, crying.

"Eilonwy – Princess," he said softly. After a moment the princess turned round.

"Hello," she said sniffing. "Flewddur is right, you know – we're going to have to work together."

"I'm grateful to you for helping me to get out of the dungeon," said Taran honestly. Eilonwy brightened. "Oh – are you? Well, we couldn't have escaped without you."

Taran felt himself blushing. "Well – er – at least we're all safe now, and–" but whatever he was about to say was lost in a great yell from amongst the trees.

"Great Beelin, help!"

"It's Flewddur," gasped Eilonwy.

"And he's in trouble!" said Taran,

running towards the trees where his friend was still bawling for all he was worth.

It was Gurgi! The little creature had jumped on Flewddur's shoulders just as he had leapt on Taran.

"Get this thing off me!" shrieked Flewddur.

Gurgi snuffled, "Gurgi want hat!"

Flewddur agreed hastily. "Have it then, quick, and go."

"Want, want, want," gurgled Gurgi happily, wearing Flewddur's hat. "Gurgi want harp."

Flewddur could hardly breathe as Gurgi yanked on the leather thong that held his harp. "Aaargh," choked Flewddur, "you're murdering me!"

"Gurgi!" shouted Taran sternly. "So it's you!"

"Master!" said Gurgi excitedly leaping towards him and letting go of the harp

35

which flew back at Flewddur and hit him smartly on the nose. Gurgi realized that he was in trouble and he hung his head. "Old man, uh – um – sit down."

"Well, I never!" said Flewddur indignantly. "Who is this pugilistic little friend of yours?"

"He's no friend of mine," said Taran staring at Flewddur's hat, which Gurgi was still wearing, "and he's a thief."

Gurgi looked pleadingly first at Taran and then at Flewddur. Then he threw back the hat, mumbling defensively, "It's too big, anyhow."

Eilonwy smiled, and Gurgi's face lit up hopefully. "What a lovely wood creature!" she said.

"Very pugilistic, too, old man said so," said Gurgi, winningly. Eilonwy giggled.

"Now go away!" ordered Taran firmly.

Gurgi loitered, dragging his feet, "Gurgi going," he said unwillingly.

Then he brightened. "Gurgi remember see piggy's footprints."

"Where?" said Taran, suspiciously.

"Today," said Gurgi, bounding up and down excitedly.

"How can you believe him?" said Flewddur.

"Don't be horrid," said Eilonwy. "He could be telling the truth."

Gurgi tugged at her skirt pleadingly. "Pretty lady, come and see."

"We'll all go," said Taran reluctantly. "But this'd better not be one of your tricks."

"Huh! I'm not trusting myself to a little hairy wood-thief," said Flewddur indignantly. "Catch me following–well–" Taran and Eilonwy had already disappeared between the trees. "Oh, drat! I suppose I'd better go and see nothing happens to them."

Gurgi was excited that at last Taran seemed pleased with him, and he ran on ahead after Hen Wen's footprints, which showed up sharp and clear in the soft ground. Suddenly the trees thinned and in front of them was a broad lake, fringed with reeds and water iris. Big flat stepping stones rose out of the lake, and as Hen Wen's footprints stopped at the first stone, it seemed that she had crossed that way.

Without pausing to think, Gurgi leapt onto the first stone, then the second, then the third. Suddenly the calm waters began to churn. Terrified, Gurgi clung to his rock, as slowly it started to revolve. It rose slightly, and then all the stones began sinking back into the lake.

"Master! Help!" squeaked Gurgi.

Taran leaned out as far as he dared, but Gurgi was now swept helplessly around in a whirlpool. His paw touched Taran, who stretched out still farther, tumbled off balance and fell into the whirling spray.

Eilonwy screamed and grabbed at his hand, but she was not strong enough to pull him to the bank, and as Flewddur tried vainly to hold her, they, too, were dragged into the seething lake. White, green, and blue water closed over Eilonwy's head, and then everything was dizzying, whirling confusion. It seemed that she was falling through a water chute, followed by the wonderful sensation of floating upwards towards the surface, surrounded by a million glittering bubbles.

This was in fact not so far from what happened. She, Taran, Flewddur and Gurgi, dazed and bewildered, lay on the sand in a cave deep under the lake. They had accidentally tumbled down one of the defences set up by the Fairfolk. The whirlpool was a rather complicated piece of fairy engineering and sometimes it went wrong. Instead of keeping people out, it sucked them down and into the realm of the Fairfolk themselves.

It was not long before they were discovered. The blue-grey gloom of the cave brightened as King Eiddileg of the Fairfolk and Old Doli, his chief engineer, second-in-command and general adviser flew towards them.

"It's perfect!" said Doli, proudly pointing to the collection of twigs and levers that was his new whirlpool device.

"Mm, yes, very good," said the King, hoping that Doli was not going to explain it to him.

"Watch!" said Doli, quite unaware that it

had been damaged. He twiddled a few knobs. Suddenly the whole contraption started to collapse.

"Watch out!" shouted the King, grabbing a stray pole before it hit him on the head. "I thought you said that this machine was supposed to keep *us* safe and *them* out!"

Through the settling dust and broken twigs King Eiddileg had seen Taran, Gurgi, Eilonwy and Flewddur. Doli was hurt and angry.

"Why do I get blamed for everything?" he said crossly. "I'm the only one who makes an effort. . ."

Eilonwy sat up. "Where am I?" she said in a dazed voice, "and – oh! Who are you?" She caught a glimpse of King Eiddileg.

"May I ask the reason for your visit?" said King Eiddileg politely.

Doli was still muttering furiously to himself. "I suppose I'm to blame for that pig as well, am I?"

"Pig!" said Taran coming to his senses immediately. "Hen Wen!"

King Eiddileg looked relieved. "Well, well, we were wondering what she was doing, but if you've come to collect her, that's very good indeed. Would you mind fetching the pig, Doli?"

Doli was not at all pleased to be sent on errands, but he obeyed, grumbling. In the shadows of the cave, dozens of curious Fairfolk had gathered to stare at the strange humans. A band of children giggled at Doli and he frowned warningly at them. The children scattered like thistledown and clustered around Eilonwy, chorusing their astonishment in tiny, musical voices.

"She's so pretty, look at her hands! Her hair is like a field of buttercups. Can she fly?"

"Oh," said Eilonwy, "you're so lovely and so tiny! I wish I *could* fly."

Suddenly a pig squealed. The Fairfolk vanished as Hen Wen scampered round a rock and leapt happily into Taran's arms.

"Well, well, I'm glad that's sorted out," said the soft voice of King Eiddileg. "Follow me to rest and have something to eat." He continued tactfully, "I imagine you have a long journey ahead?"

It was a delicious meal. Afterwards, Taran explained their quest for the Black Cauldron.

"The Black Cauldron!" exclaimed the King frowning. "So that's what he's after. For some time now we have stopped our travels amongst humans. It is too dangerous for us; and too sad to see the suffering and horror which has come to your land. But if the Horned King finds the Black Cauldron, no one will be safe."

"Then I must find the Cauldron and destroy it," said Taran.

"That will not be easy," said the King seriously. "It is in the Marshes of Morva. Doli knows where it is. He will take you."

"Will you come with me too, Eilonwy?" asked Taran gently.

"I'll come," said Eilonwy, "But how will you destroy the Black Cauldron when you find it?"

"We'll find a way," said Taran.

"Don't forget me," said Flewddur, a little hurt, "*I'm* coming."

"And Gurgi too, master," said Gurgi, anxious to get on land again.

"Well, well, that's settled then," said King Eiddileg with satisfaction. He put his hand under his cloak and pulled out a handful of sparkling fairy-dust which he scattered over the four of them. Suddenly they felt themselves rising through the air.

"Hen Wen!" shouted Taran as the Fairfolk were rapidly disappearing. "Please look after her!"

"Don't worry," called King Eiddileg. We'll get her home safely for you."

Perhaps the friends would not have felt so reassured if they had seen what was happening at the Castle of the Horned King.

Like obedient, evil shadows, the Gwythaints had returned home to their master to tell him the news they had gathered.

"So," said the Horned King," they want to destroy the Cauldron?" He laughed. "How very helpful to us. Go," he ordered Creeper, "and do not fail!"

The Horned King was excited. He could not rest. Success seemed so very close. He opened the door of the Secret Chamber. The skeletons of dead soldiers rattled gently in the draught. Lovingly, the Horned King fondled a skull. "My soldiers," he murmured. "Soon, your time will come. I will make you *Cauldron Born*. Then, yes,

then, you will worship me." He raised his arms exultantly. "Then I shall be a god amongst mortal men. None will be able to stand against me!"

Meanwhile, Taran and his friends struggled on towards the Marshes of Morva. They had long since left the sunny forest and the safety of the Lake of Fairfolk. It grew cold and wet. Soft green grass made way for stones and grey mud and the few stunted trees that struggled to grow looked defeated and sad.

Eilonwy shivered. "What a place!" she said in a small voice.

"Are you sure that this is right, Doli?" said Flewddur uncertainly.

"Of course I'm sure," said Doli irritated. "Isn't that just like humans? They would doubt that today was Monday unless someone showed them the calendar."

"I think it's Tuesday," said Flewddur. "*I* think that we've – oops!" He slipped on the wet ground and skidded down a slope.

"Stupid oaf!" muttered Doli. At the foot of the slope was a tumble-down cottage, so overgrown that it was hard to believe that anyone lived there. Windows stared out blankly through a tangle of ivy and dead creepers.

"Here you are," said Doli in an off-hand fashion. "This is where you'll find the Cauldron."

"We'd better go in," said Taran without enthusiasm.

Gurgi huddled close to Eilonwy. "Gurgi not like this place. *Nooo,*" he whispered.

Inside, it was very dark, but there was just enough light for them to see all kinds of unpleasant things hanging from the ceiling, and resting in cobwebby nooks and crannies. A dead bat brushed against Eilonwy's cheek and she shuddered. Blindly, they stumbled about the room, opening cupboards and drawers, unaware that dozens of cold eyes were watching their every move. A skull slipped and shattered at Flewddur's feet. They all jumped nervously.

"This is hopeless," said Eilonwy. "We don't even know where to start looking for this thing."

"It must be here somewhere," said Taran, a little desperately, lifting the catch on an enormous trunk and throwing open the lid.

Suddenly, a thousand frogs leapt out at him, croaking wildly, and knocking him over. Eilonwy screamed in terror as they surrounded her, hopping on her arms and face. Then they saw the open door and almost as abruptly as they had arrived, they streamed out, hopping and leaping to freedom.

"Why, they're only frogs!" said Taran, laughing with relief.

"Those were people," said Doli, soberly.

"You mean – they were turned into frogs?" said Taran; but this unpleasant thought did not have time to sink in, for just at that moment, there was a terrible scream.

"Thieves! Thieves!" The terrifying voice echoed round the room. Taran, Eilonwy and Flewddur took one startled look at each other and moved towards the door. Billowing smoke blocked their way and the curling mist cleared to show three ancient spirits, the witches Orgoch, Orwen and Orddu. Orddu spoke first, her eyes in the thick folds of leathery skin as bright and cold as a snake. "Wicked people! You shall all be turned into frogs and eaten."

"Come to think of it," said Orgoch, "you look nice and tender," and she bared her yellow teeth.

Flewddur backed away, pulling the others with him. "Er, well, ladies, so sorry to disturb you, but we must be going." But before they could move, a fat, warty hand seized him by the shoulder. It was Orwen.

"Mm," she said coyly. "Aren't you the masterful one!"

"W-Who?" stammered Flewddur.

Orwen's fat lips nuzzled his arm. "I'm just what you've been looking for, aren't I?" she cooed.

Flewddur looked round wildly. "Er – yes! Very attractive," he mumbled.

Orgoch was annoyed at this interruption and she raised a skinny finger and pointed it at the poet. A green flash zipped through the air – and Flewddur vanished. Sitting on the floor, croaking dismally, was a wiry green frog.

"How's that?" crowed Orgoch. "Just in time for supper, too." She grabbed at the frog, who slithered out of her grasp. Orddu cackled with laughter.

"Stop grinning and help me!" ordered Orgoch. Three pairs of hands snatched at thin air as Flewddur-frog leapt desperately out of their reach. He overbalanced and Orgoch swept him straight into a bubbling pan of stew.

"Gotcha!" yelled Orgoch happily. She scooped him out with a spoon and sprinkled him with salt. "I do love frog–"

"He's mine!" screamed Orwen furiously shoving Orgoch out of the way. "There, there, come to Orwen, my love," she crooned.

44

The poor poet, drenched and confused, found himself half smothered in the witch's heaving bosom.

"Hey, where are you? Help! Find him! I'll never, ever forgive you, Orgoch!" yelped Orwen as the frog tumbled down her cleavage and onto the floor. She pointed a plump finger at Flewddur. Again there was a green flash, as the poet found himself back in his normal shape. He opened his mouth as a fly buzzed past and then snapped it shut again, quite embarrassed.

Taking advantage of all the confusion, Taran had found his sword. He drew it and pointed it at the three hags. "Enough!" he shouted. "We've come for the Black Cauldron!" The witches fell silent.

"*Ssso,*" hissed Orgoch "You want the Cauldron? No one has asked for that in two thousand years." She laughed unpleasantly. "But maybe I could interest you in something else–" she opened another door in the cottage.

Suddenly a host of pots, pans, kettles, buckets and jars came flying out like a squadron of fighter planes. They circled Taran and dived in to attack before he realized what was happening. The sword went flying as a teapot hit him on the head and he fell over backwards.

"Well, see anything you like?" sneered Orgoch. Her face dropped however, as the sword suddenly leapt into the air, thrust itself hilt-first into Taran's outstretched hand, and began slicing up the attacking pots, which cowered and fled. As if berserk, it dragged Taran through the cottage, chopping and slashing until all the utensils were smashed or in hiding.

"Did you see that, Orddu!" said Orgoch, awestruck.

"I've never seen a sword like it!" said Orwen, trembling.

"And I want it!" said Orddu firmly. "We'll have to bargain."

Orddu smiled at Taran, rather like a crocodile, thought Eilonwy. "Listen, young man," she said. "you can have the Cauldron–" she raised her hand at Flewddur's excited gasp, "–in return for that old sword of yours."

Taran looked disconsolate. "I'm not giving up my sword."

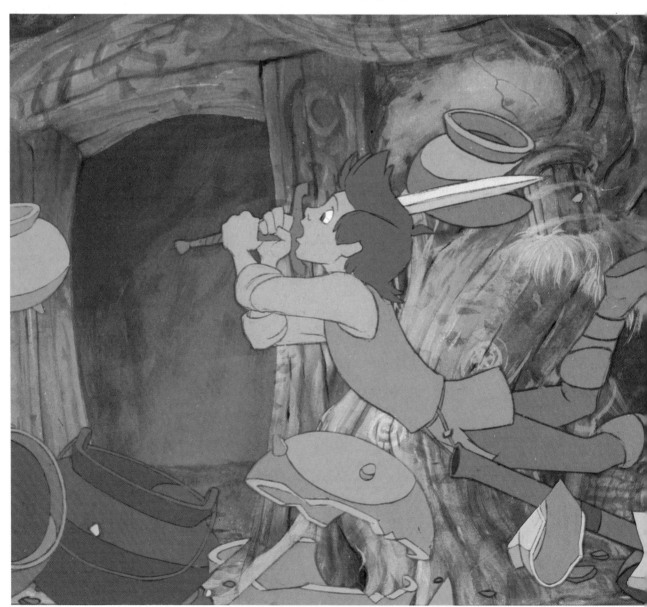

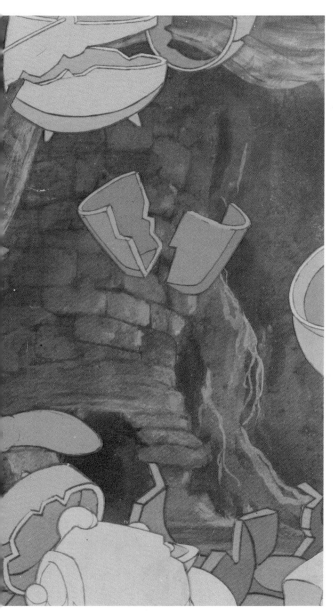

Orddu grinned maliciously. "Please yourself, but we *never* give anything away. We bargain."

Flewddur took a deep breath. "Madam – would you consider taking this very fine harp for your Cauldron?"

Orddu laughed derisively, "Harp! I hate music."

"Would my magic bubble do in exchange?" offered Eilonwy pleadingly.

"Don't be silly," scoffed Orddu. "I've got more magic bubbles than I know what to do with."

Gurgi lifted up his open paw. It was full of wriggly insects. "Munchings and crunchings?" he said. "Gurgi will trade them."

"Hm–" interrupted Orgoch, snatching up the insects and dropping them into her mouth, "not bad."

"But not a bargain, I think," grinned Orddu. Taran's face set hard. "You strike a hard bargain," he said, "but I will let you have my dearest possession, my sword, in return for the Cauldron."

Orddu's eyes gleamed. "You give up the sword, willingly?" she questioned.

"No, Taran, no!" cried Eilonwy.

"I must give it up," said Taran quietly.

"Then," laughed Orddu triumphantly, "it's a bargain." She raised her arms and muttered the words of an ancient spell. The room filled with crackling light and suddenly the sword disappeared from Taran's hand.

47

The lights dimmed and the witches vanished. A terrific wind seemed to be sucking everything away. Pots, pans, chairs, dead rats, hurled past them as the hurricane began to tear the cottage apart as easily as a piece of card. The roof collapsed as if crushed by something heavy. "Watch out!" screamed Eilonwy. A squadron of flying pots streamed past, smashing everything in its path. Taran, Eilonwy, Flewddur and Gurgi threw themselves to the ground. The earth creaked and groaned terrifyingly beneath them as if it was splitting apart. Steam spurted out of the rocks which shuddered violently, as something huge and black heaved itself out of the ground.

The friends watched awestruck.

"The Cauldron," whispered Taran. "And it's ours!"

They ran towards it. It was carved with strange ciphers and runes whose meaning none of them, even Doli, could begin to guess.

"Quick!" ordered Taran. "We must destroy it." He picked up a broken branch and struck the Cauldron with all his strength. The stick snapped, but the Cauldron remained unscratched. They rolled a huge rock against the Cauldron; which obstinately remained unharmed. An hour later, they had to admit defeat.

"We *will* smash you," cried Taran, almost in tears, beating his fist against the black metal.

A horrid mocking laugh rang out. It was Orgoch, watching from a cloud above them.

"Didn't you know the Cauldron was indestructible?" she jeered.

"You didn't tell us!" cried Taran, "that's not fair."

Orddu's head appeared and she giggled. "Fair? We're not supposed to be fair. . . We had a bargain remember? You have the Cauldron. It's not our fault you can't do anything with it."

"Now, look here, madam," shouted Flewddur, "that sword won't be any use to you if you play tricks like this. We made a bargain honourably. You know we have to destroy the Cauldron."

"There is a way," said Orwen, smiling fatly. "–but I forget it."

"Of course there's a way," said Orddu briskly, leaning out of her cloud towards them, her hair streaming in the wind. "Now listen to me, you silly little geese. The Black Cauldron can never be *destroyed*, but its evil powers can be *stopped*. A living being must, of his own free will, climb into the Cauldron." She paused.

Gurgi bounded forward. "Gurgi is bold and brave. He is not afraid to climb." He scrambled up onto the rim of the Cauldron.

"Of course," continued Orddu calmly, "the poor wretch *will never climb out alive.*" She cackled as Gurgi shrank back to the ground. "Too bad, my little geese, too bad. Next time perhaps a real hero will come for the Cauldron. . ."

49

Screaming with laughter the witches vanished, but, faintly on the wind, Taran heard Orgoch's parting shot, "*if* there's a next time."

Taran sat down on a log and put his head in his hands. Eilonwy put her arm round him.

"I've let you down," he mumbled. "Without that sword I'm just a pig-keeper."

Doli could stand it no longer. He was furious. "You stupid, stupid, human! Nothing ever works out when you're dealing with people. I can't think why I wasted my time coming here with you!" And with one angry shake of his wings he vanished in a puff of fairy dust.

"We're better off without him," said Eilonwy consolingly. "I don't think he ever realized how serious our mission is."

"And we've failed!" said Taran bitterly. "Doli is right. I *was* stupid."

"Listen," said Eilonwy softly. "*I* believe in you."

"Y-you do?" said Taran, brightening.

"I think that you're – well – you're–" he looked into her eyes and her voice trailed away. He took her hand and squeezed it gently. Suddenly there was a splutter of disgust from Flewddur. Gurgi had been so upset at the sight of Taran's misery that he leapt on Flewddur and licked his chin.

"Yuk," cried the poet. "Get off, you misplaced hearth rug."

Taran laughed. His despair had passed.

"Come on!" he said, "You've been true friends. Now it's up to me." A shadow passed over the moon, Gurgi whimpered; he

ran and hid. Gwythaints! Eilonwy screamed as the creatures swooped, their claws outstretched.

"Quick!" shouted Taran, "they mustn't catch us!" But his way was barred by a huge spear. They were surrounded by henchmen of the Horned King.

"You won't escape this time," sneered Creeper. No one saw Gurgi's frightened eyes peeping out from the leaves, as Taran, Eilonwy and Flewddur were led away.

The iron-studded door clanged shut on the hideous Secret Chamber. A cart, loaded with skeletons, rumbled into the room, its grisly cargo clattering like so many gruesome puppets. Taran, Eilonwy and Flewddur, tied by their wrists to a high beam in the roof, looked down at the Black Cauldron, where it squatted on a raised platform, like an evil creature. With a show of mock politeness, Creeper bowed low to them. "Was it the Cauldron you were looking for?" he sneered. "How fortunate you are! You will be given the opportunity to serve His Majesty, the Horned King. You will become one of his slaves, one of the *Cauldron Born.*" He sniggered. *"Heh-heh-heh.* Everything is ready, Sire."

The Horned King had appeared on the platform. He smiled faintly at Taran; but his eyes were as empty of feeling as two black holes. "Perhaps you would like to see the power of the Black Cauldron," he whispered. "You are privileged to watch the awakening of my Army of the Dead." Powerfully, he seized one of the skeletons, and with one swift movement hurled it into the Cauldron. "Arise!" he cried. "Arise, my messengers of Death; our time has come!"

Slowly, a pale mist curled out of the Cauldron. The mist grew thicker, seething and boiling. A few drops of blood appeared

on the lip of the Cauldron and trickled onto the floor in an ever-growing stream. Horror-struck, Taran watched as blood and ectoplasmic slime began pouring into the Chamber, drowning the tangled heaps of bones. Jerkily, the bones quivered, as if some ghastly animator was bringing them to life. Dead eye sockets gleamed faintly and boney skeletal hands clutched out of the mist for their unseen weapons. The slime heaved and shuddered, as if giving birth, and the luminous glow became stronger. Taran, Eilonwy and Flewddur were not alone in their terror. The guards stood, rooted to the spot.

Then hordes of living skeletons rose from the mist, their eyeless skulls turned towards some unseen goal. "Go forth, my beloved warriors," hissed the Horned King. "Destroy all living things!"

Those guards who still had power of movement ran shrieking from the castle, followed by a never-ending stream of Cauldron Born, marching implacably forwards on their mission of destruction.

"Come," said the Horned King to Creeper. "We shall watch this moment of my greatest triumph from the tower."

Meanwhile, what had been happening to Gurgi? Bravely, the little creature had followed his captured friends into the castle. He climbed the stairs and paused in an alcove, as a couple of frightened guards pounded past. Then he heard the terrifying clatter of a million boney feet on stone floors – and he panicked and ran, whimpering with fear. A small grating blocked his path and he paused; but what he saw through the bars made him gasp, his fright forgotten. "Master!" he cried, happily.

"Gurgi!" shouted Taran. "How did you find us!" Gurgi slipped through the grating, ran along the beam and began biting through the ropes that tied Taran.

"Gurgi sorry he runs away," he mumbled through the strands of rope, "but we will all leave this evil place."

Taran shook his wrists to bring back the circulation. "Listen, Flewddur. You and Eilonwy escape as quickly as possible. I *must* stop the Cauldron before it's too late."

"Taran, no!" cried Eilonwy. "We're in this together, remember?"

"Not this time," said Taran firmly. "It's my fault that the Horned King captured the Cauldron. It's up to me to stop its power." He began crawling along the edge of the archway above the still steaming Cauldron.

"Listen, Taran," shouted Flewddur. "There must be another way. . ." Taran shook his head, not trusting himself to reply, and continued crawling towards his goal.

Whining, Gurgi scrambled after him.

"Wait, Master! Wait for Gurgi!" His paws slipped and dislodged a few stones which fell and exploded into the boiling Cauldron.

Gurgi shivered. "Please, Master, not go into evil Cauldron," he pleaded.

Taran tried to push him aside. "Listen, Gurgi, if I don't, we're all going to die, anyway."

Gurgi stopped, muttering to himself. "Taran has many friends. . .Gurgi has no friends." Taking a deep breath, he scuttled past Taran to the edge of the broken arch.

"No!" screamed Taran. "Gurgi!" But it was too late. Tumbling over and over, the brave little creature fell headlong into the Cauldron below. There was a tremendous flash of light, as the Cauldron was wracked by some ghastly internal explosion.

"Look!" shouted Eilonwy. "It's losing it's power!" Slowly but with gathering speed, the Cauldron was sucking the mists and ectoplasmic slime back into itself.

Outside, the horrific army of Cauldron Born faltered and fell. Skeletons collapsed where they stood and tumbled into the moat.

"Sire, sire, what's h-happening?" stuttered Creeper. "The Army is *dying!*"

"It can't be!" screamed the Horned King hysterically. "This is the moment of my greatest triumph. I must have supreme power!"

The skeletons were disintegrating even before they reached the drawbridge, and from inside the castle came an ominous rumbling sound as the Cauldron continued to suck its vapours back into itself.

"It's hungry. It needs another body," cried the Horned King, his eyes gleaming maniacally. "Yours!" He grabbed the cowering Creeper by the throat.

Flewddur and Eilonwy were still trying to persuade Taran to save himself. "You must come, Taran," cried Eilonwy. "Gurgi would have wanted it."

"No!" said Taran, walking towards the Cauldron. "He was braver than I was. Maybe there's still a chance I can save him – *aah!*" He had entered the force field of the Cauldron. Slipping and sliding, he was dragged towards it. He put out his hand to save himself and his fingers closed round an iron ring in a pillar. He clung to it with all his strength.

Behind him, he could hear Creeper screaming, "No! No! Please, Sire!" The Horned King was demented by the failure of his plans and he had one thought only in his mind – vengeance. Skeletons scattered in his path, harmless heaps of bones and he kicked them into a thousand splinters. "Get up, you cowards! Kill!" he screamed.

"Look," cried Creeper desperately. "The Pig Boy! It's all his fault."
The Horned King's eyes glowed. "You have interfered for the very last time," he hissed at Taran, tossing the dwarf aside. "You shall die, pig-keeper. . .horribly." A claw like steel seized Taran by the shoulder.

Wrenching him from the ring, the King lifted the boy like a feather and hurled him into the air. Taran tumbled over and over until he struck the steps at the foot of the Cauldron. There he lay, half-dazed, with the sound of the gusty winds roaring in his ears. Eilonwy and Flewddur could only watch, helplessly.

"Pig Boy, you shall satisfy the Cauldron's hunger," screeched the Horned King. Crazed with hate, he moved towards the Cauldron; but a swirling gust of vapour caught him off balance and he found himself being drawn irresistibly towards it. "You'll not get me," jeered the Horned King. "I cannot die!"

The Cauldron glowed and a face of horrifying evil showed briefly on the surface of the metal. Struggling desperately with the Cauldron's power, real terror showed on the King's face. "I curse you. I curse you for ever. *NO – AAAGH!*" He was hurled against the Cauldron's side and a scream of terrible pain broke from his lips. Slowly, his hands began to disintegrate and soon there was nothing but a twist of smokey vapour clinging to the empty rim.

Creeper's eyes bulged with incredulity. He began giggling hysterically, "Oh-h, no! How horrible! He's gone for good. . ." and he fled, still gurgling with insane laughter.

The Cauldron continued to roar and rumble, churning restlessly. It began glowing with white-hot intensity. Taran came out of his daze. The floor around him was cracking with the heat. He ran, as steam began pouring out of the stones. "Eilonwy! Flewddur!" he cried. The ceiling bulged. Flewddur and Eilonwy were huddled in a doorway. They ran towards him and hugged him.

"Thank goodness you're safe!" cried Eilonwy. Rocks showered down on them from all sides as the walls sagged. "Hurry!" shouted Flewddur. "The castle's collapsing."

Breath caught in their throats as they raced along the corridors. "The bridge!" panted Taran. Behind them, there was a tremendous crash, followed by the sound of cracking wood and stone. The floor of the Chamber of the Dead had fallen through. A horrible screaming told them that the Gwythaints, chained to their perches, had been sucked through the floor with the Cauldron. A sheet of flame leapt up through the centre of the castle.

Taran reached the drawbridge. A crack appeared in front of him and he leapt across. Eilonwy paused. It widened to a chasm, and taking a deep breath, she, too, leapt to safety, followed almost immediately by Flewddur. With a splintering crash, the drawbridge collapsed, a buckled mass of wood and iron. "The moat!" gasped Taran. The three friends ran down the step to the water. To their relief, an old canal boat was still moored there. It had been used by the Horned King to ferry his prisoners secretly to the castle. The boat was rocking dangerously, as the three of them clambered in. "Push her off, Flewddur," shouted Taran. The poet untied the mooring ropes and then paused.

"Oh, no!" he mumbled. There in front of them was the water gate – and it was shut!

The boat bumped against the metal bars of the gate, as stones and burning wood rained down on them from above. Taran stood up in the boat an began struggling with the rusty chain that held the gate. "Hurry!" begged Eilonwy, as Taran slowly began to drag the gate open. The force of water pushed them against the gate as they attempted to steer the boat through the narrow opening. Flewddur glanced up. "LOOK OUT!" he shrieked. A huge column of stone had broken off the castle and was hurtling towards them. An avalanche of rock hit the water next to the boat, which leapt like a deer over the gate, tossed by the tidal wave.

"Hold on!" cried Taran amid the crashing, foaming water. They had escaped! Behind them, with a tremendous roar, the castle wall collapsed into the moat. Gigantic smoke clouds billowed into the sky and the air was full of whirling sparks.

"Whew!" said Taran, shaking the water out of his eyes. "We did it!" The three friends were hanging on to what remained of the old canal boat. They paddled themselves towards the bank.

Over everything hung a dismal pall of dark smoke, and from where the castle had once stood, an occasional greedy flame still licked upwards to the sky. The Horned King was gone forever.

"Taran, look!" said Eilonwy pointing. Floating quietly on the water was the Black Cauldron. The memory of Gurgi flooded back to Taran and he found himself crying bitterly.

"Why did I let him do it?" he muttered. "I should have been the one to jump. . ."
Very gently, Flewddur lifted Taran out of the water and laid the boy on the bank. The poet patted him reassuringly on the shoulder. "Listen, Taran, it wasn't your fault," he said.
There was a dry cough from somewhere above them. It was the witches, Orwen, Orgoch and Orddu, hovering in the thick clouds over the Cauldron.

"What is the matter with the poor little goose?" cackled Orgoch.

"He got what he wanted didn't he?" added Orddu.

"What do you want this time, ladies?" said Flewddur in a challenging voice.

"We have business with your little hero," said Orddu haughtily.

Taran looked up, miserably. "Hero? I'm no hero."

Orddu put on her most sugary voice, "We know you don't need it any more so–" Orwen and Orgoch vanished, to reappear,

panting, with the Cauldron, which they balanced on their cloud. "We'll just take it and be on our way."

In a flash Flewddur realized what was happening. "Not so fast," he commanded. "That Cauldron belongs to Taran. Do you remember? And *we* never give anything away. We bargain."

Orddu pulled a face and signalled to the other two, who dropped the Cauldron with a splash into the water. "Did you say 'bargain'?" said Orddu.

"I most certainly did," said Flewddur with growing confidence. "Come on, now, what will you give us?"

There was a green flash and Taran's sword hovered in the air in front of him, glowing faintly.

"Take it then," urged Orgoch.

"No!" said Taran flatly. The witches gasped in astonishment. "I don't need a sword like that," he continued.

Orddu grinned in triumph and the sword vanished with a green flash, only to reappear in her skinny hand.

"However, I will trade the Cauldron for my friend Gurgi." The witches looked momentarily confused.

"Oh dear!" said Orwen. "That's not possible," said Orddu angrily.

"It's *old* Magic, you know," said Orgoch. "No one is meant to interfere!"

"Just as I thought, madam," said Flewddur maliciously, "you have no real power, admit it!" The witches flew into a towering rage.

"No power!" shrieked Orgoch.

"We'll show him," screamed Orddu. They went whirling through the air like Catherine wheels, coloured sparks flying wildly until they seemed to dissolve into brilliant colour: red, green, yellow.

They surrounded the Cauldron, which rose in the air like a feather. There was a blinding flash of pure, white light that seemed to shoot in a spiral far beyond the clouds. Orddu's voice, far above them, sounded unearthly, "We have made a bargain. . ." she cackled. Witches and Cauldron disappeared and a small, spinning whirlwind remained, stirring the grasses at the water's edge. The whirlwind settled, slowly fading away, and the tiny, still form of

Gurgi lay crumpled on the ground.

A lump in his throat, Taran picked him up in his arms. A tear rolled down his cheek. Eilonwy was crying, quietly, beside him, and Flewddur shuffled his feet uncomfortably. He did not trust himself to speak. Gently, Taran gave the little creature a hug – and Gurgi put his paw on Taran's vest.

"Gurgi!" yelled Taran, almost dropping him with delight. "You're alive!" Gurgi shook himself in excitement and disbelief.

"Look! Gurgi alive! No pains, no hurt. Gurgi's ALIVE."

The four of them hugged each other as if they never wanted to let go.

Gurgi put Eilonwy's hand into Taran's and jumped down.

"You clever little thing," laughed Eilonwy, but she did not take her hand away. Gurgi giggled proudly, eyeing Taran, who had not taken his hand away either.

"Gurgi's happy day," he crowed.

"Let's all go home," said Taran.

"Home?" said Eilonwy and Flewddur questioningly.

"We'll all go back to Caer Dallben together," said Taran. "I bet Hen Wen has already told Dallben that we're coming."

At that very moment, Dallben and Hen Wen were making plans for the best homecoming Taran had ever had.

PRINTED IN BELGIUM BY
proost
INTERNATIONAL BOOK PRODUCTION